WALT DISNEY

Lady
and the Tramp

Longmeadow Press

It was Christmas Eve in London, many many years ago. The streets and houses were covered with freshly fallen snow. Lights burned brightly in the windows, and the air tingled with excitement. Soon it would be time to open the presents.

At last, the clock struck midnight.

At Jim Dear and Darling's home, many colorful boxes lay under the Christmas tree. "Here, open this one first," said Jim Dear, handing Darling a large box.

"What is it?" asked Darling.

"Open it and you'll see," said Jim Dear, smiling.

Darling had barely undone the ribbon, when out jumped a cocker spaniel puppy. "Oh. He's so cute!" cried Darling.

"It's a she, and her name is Lady," corrected Jim Dear.

Lady soon became the queen of the household. She
was pampered and petted by everyone. And in return,
she looked after the couple, fetching Jim Dear's
newspaper and slippers and guarding the house at night.
For her birthday she received a beautiful blue collar.
"Look at how pretty you are," said Darling.
"Wait till the others see me," thought Lady.

Jock, the Scottish terrier and Trusty, the bloodhound, were her neighbors. They were purebreds, too, and very distinguished.

Trusty was once a brilliant detective. But he had grown old and his nose wasn't what it used to be.

"What a beautiful collar!" they exclaimed. "You've grown into a lovely little Lady."

But although Lady enjoyed her pampered life, one day she noticed that things had slowly begun to change. No one seemed to pay much attention to her anymore. She didn't understand what was happening.

"What have I done wrong?" she asked herself. "This afternoon, Jim Dear rushed by without even giving me a pat on the head. And Darling spends all her time knitting. She hasn't taken me for a walk in ages. And what's all this talk about a 'happy event'?"

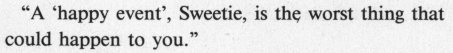

"A 'happy event', Sweetie, is the worst thing that could happen to you."

Lady looked around in alarm. "Who's that dog?" she thought indignantly. "Look at that scruffy beast! And, he's not wearing a collar. How dare that common mongrel even talk to me!"

"It's a cinch!" said the
mongrel. "Your mistress is
going to have a baby! Soon
some brat is going to be
pulling your tail and
jumping on your back!
Listen to me, Sweetie. Leave
that fancy collar behind and
skedaddle out of here!"

"So long and good luck!"
he said with a wink, and was
gone in a flash.

Tramp, the mongrel, was right. Within a few days the house was buzzing with activity. People came and went, bringing presents and making funny noises over a crib.

Lady was allowed to see the baby. "He's not so awful," she thought. "In fact, he's rather cute. Perhaps we'll be friends."

Soon everything was back to normal, but not for long. One day a fierce-looking woman with a suitcase came to the door

"Lady, this is Aunt Sarah," said Darling. "She's going to look after the baby while Jim Dear and I take a little vacation."

With Aunt Sarah came two Siamese cats. Those two monsters took over the house in no time.

Si and Am were their names. They were crafty and bold. "We are Siamese if you please! We are Siamese if you don't please! Hah! Hah! Hah!" they sneered. "Where we come from Cats are Kings. Death to all dogs!" The cats slinked around poor Lady.

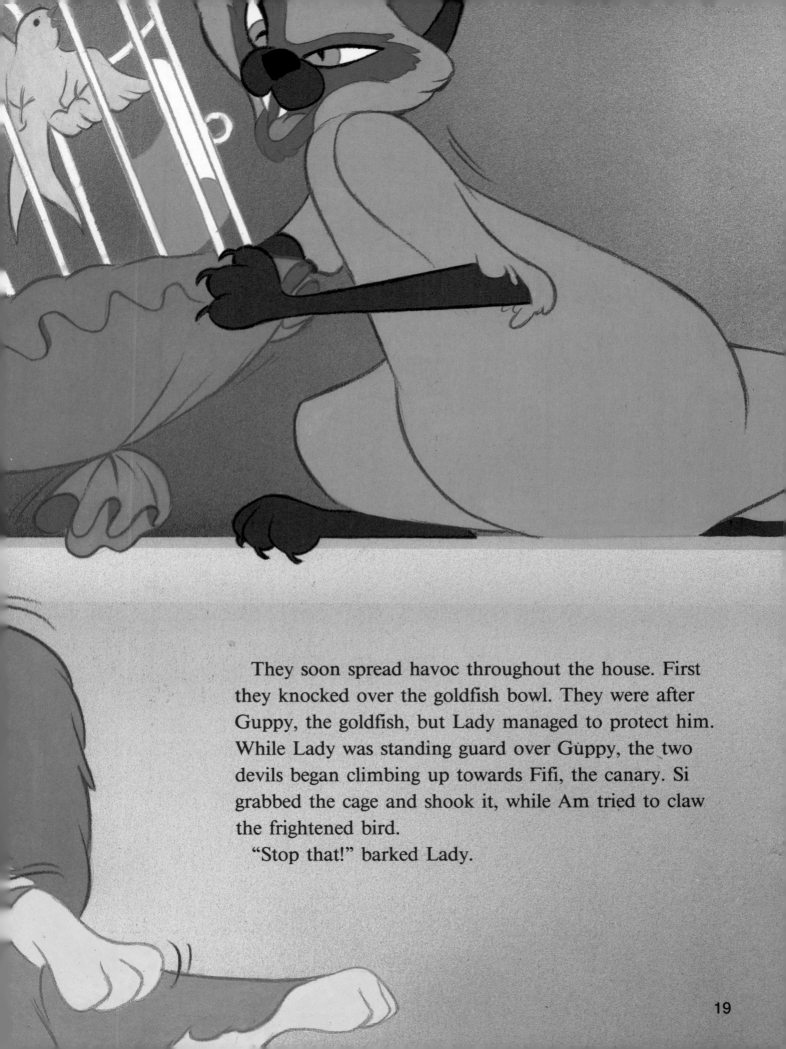

They soon spread havoc throughout the house. First they knocked over the goldfish bowl. They were after Guppy, the goldfish, but Lady managed to protect him. While Lady was standing guard over Guppy, the two devils began climbing up towards Fifi, the canary. Si grabbed the cage and shook it, while Am tried to claw the frightened bird.

"Stop that!" barked Lady.

CRAAASSSHH! BAANNGG! The cage fell, knocking over a painting on its way.

Aunt Sarah came rushing into the room. "What's this?" she demanded pointing at the mess. Si and Am purred sweetly, pretending innocence. Aunt Sarah glared at Lady. "You naughty dog! You'll be punished for this!" she threatened as she carried off her two cats. "My poor babies. You musn't play with that wicked dog," she cooed into their ears.

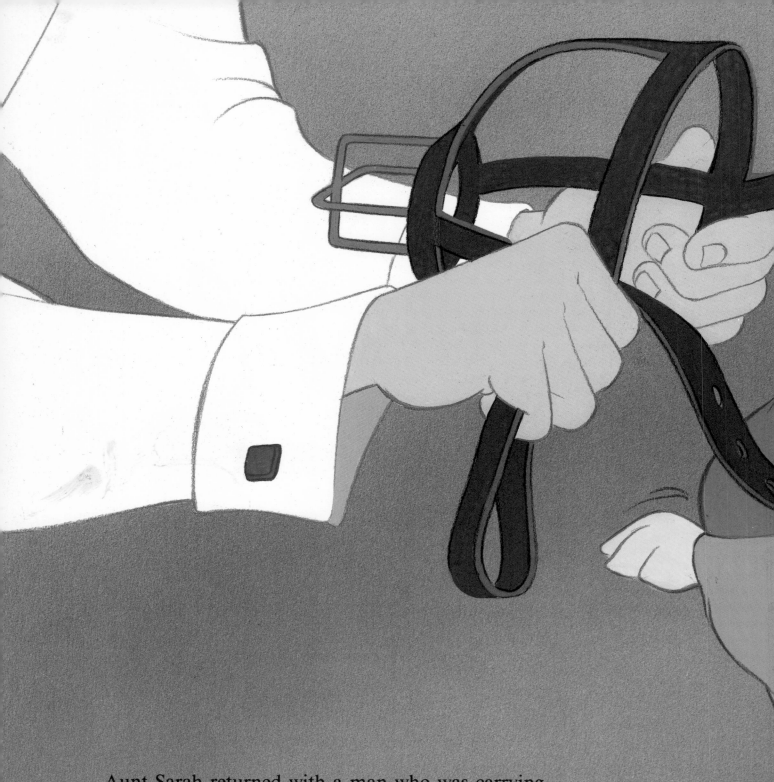

Aunt Sarah returned with a man who was carrying
something. Aunt Sarah grabbed Lady and held her
tightly while the man put a leather mask over her face.
  "A muzzle!" cried Lady. "What are they doing to me?
Oh! I wish that Jim Dear and Darling were here." Lady
squirmed out of Aunt Sarah's arms and fled out of
the house.

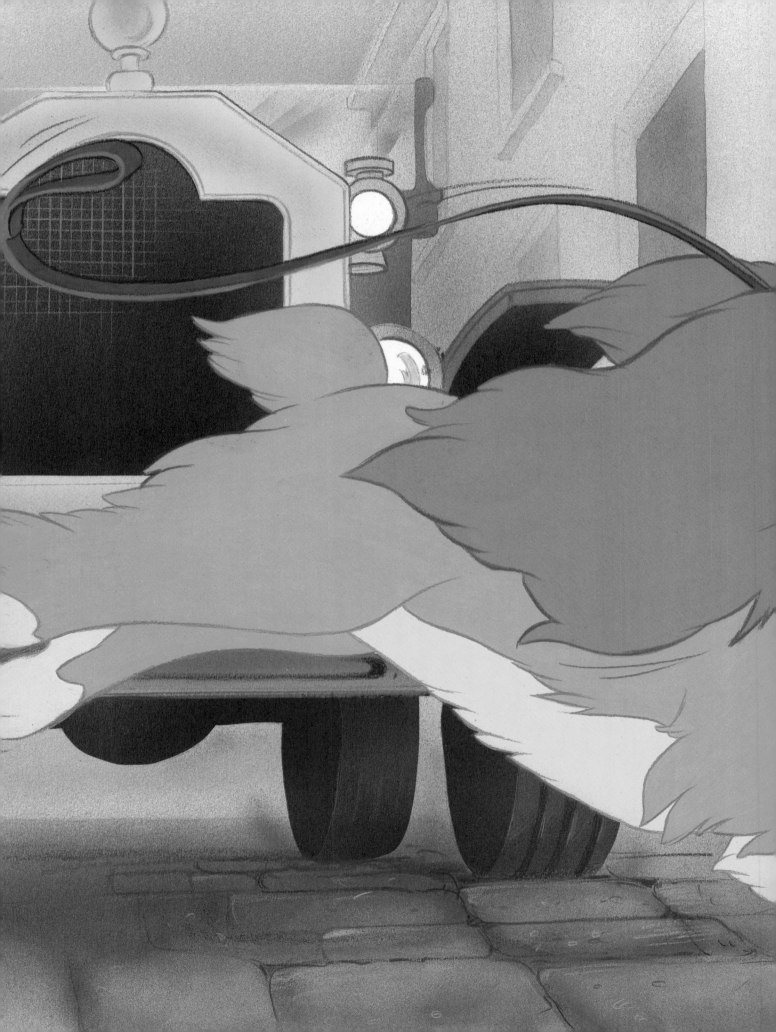

Poor Lady was so horrified
that she ran without really
watching where she was
going.

She rushed in between
passing cars and crowded
streets. She wanted to get as
far away from that woman
as possible.

A gang of stray dogs, seeing her dash by, started to chase after her. Wearing her muzzle she'd be easy game for them. Hearing the dogs behind her, Lady ran even faster.

Tramp, who was nearby, heard the dogs and turned just in time to see what was happening. "Poor little devil!" he said. " I'd better go and help her out!" He dashed after the dogs.

When Tramp caught up with the dogs he saw that Lady was cornered by two snarling beasts.

"Aren't you guys ashamed of yourselves? Picking on a defenseless creature!" snarled Tramp, leaping to the rescue. "Scram you two—before I make hamburger meat out of you!"

"It's Tramp!" barked one of the bullies. "Let's get out of here!" They slunk off with their tails between their legs.

"Hi there, Sweetheart! Tramp at your service. King of the mutts and Prince of the mongrels. Always ready for a scuffle." Tramp peered at Lady closely. "Hey, haven't I seen you before?" he asked, pricking up his ears.

Poor Lady couldn't speak—not with the muzzle on her. "I've got it!" shouted Tramp. "You're the little dame whose mistress was having a baby! What are you doing so far from home? And who put that contraption on you?"

Tramp realized that Lady could hardly answer him
with her jaws locked up. "Follow me, Sweetie! We'll
have that thing off you in a jiffy." Tramp led her to
the Zoo.

They stopped at Mr. Croc's cage. "This should do it.
Just stick your nose through these bars," advised Tramp.
But Lady didn't like that gleam in Mr Croc's eyes.
He looked more hungry than helpful.

Seeing Lady back away in fear, Tramp decided to look for another solution. Soon they came across Busy the Beaver, who was hard at work.

"Hi there, Busy! How about giving us a hand—or should I say tooth?" chuckled Tramp.

Busy waddled up to Lady and looked her over. "Hmm. Let me see. Oh this should be no problem. A few gnaws here and there, and we'll have that muzzle off in no time."

Busy knew his job. His sharp teeth gnawed furiously
until "SNAP!" off came the muzzle.

"Oh really, Mr Beaver," said Lady. "I don't know how
I can ever thank you!" She wagged her tail in gratitude.

"Think nothing of it. It was my pleasure," replied
Busy Beaver with a gracious bow.

"And now I bet you're hungry, Sweetie. Come on, I'll treat you to dinner. I hope you like Italian food." Tramp guided Lady to the back of a little Italian restaurant.

"Trrammp, watta gooda suprisa!" beamed Tony the chef. "And who's your *bella fidanzata*?"

"What's a *bella fidanzata*?" thought Lady.

Tony was a real romantic. Soon he had the two dogs eating spaghetti by candlelight. And while they ate he played his accordian and sang love songs. This was all very new to Lady. She was enjoying it. And she told Tramp everything, about the baby, the Siamese cats and Aunt Sarah.

After dinner, Tramp took Lady for a stroll in the park. There was a full moon. "He's really not so bad," thought Lady. "He's not a purebred, like me, but there's something about special him."

The two dogs fell asleep under the stars. Each dreamed of the other.

Lady woke with a start. The sun had risen. It was late. "I must go home now!" said Lady. "Everyone will be wondering where I am."

"What's wrong, Sweetie? Don't you like the outdoor life?"

"Yes, but my masters."

"No masters—no kennels—no chains! That's my motto!" said Tramp, running beside her.

Tramp stopped suddenly. "Do you hear what I hear? Chickens! That means eggs. Now for our breakfast." And before Lady could stop him, Tramp dived into the midst of the clucking hens.

"Stop! Don't do that!" cried Lady. "Someone will catch you." But Tramp was having too much fun.

PIINNGG! Bullets began to fly.

"Run for it Sweetie. Someone's shooting at us," yelled Tramp.

"I knew he'd get caught," thought Lady. "And look at him laughing. He thinks this is just a joke."

Tramp ran on ahead and disappeared around the corner.

"Wait for me, Tramp!" begged Lady.

Tramp was too far ahead to hear Lady's cries. When Lady stopped to catch her breath, a truck screeched to a halt. Two men jumped out and grabbed her. "There's the thief!" one of them cried. "Caught redhanded. Look! There are feathers in her hair."

Before she knew what was happening, Lady found herself behind bars at the city dog pound. Never had she seen so many mangy-looking dogs. Tears began to gather in her eyes.

"Oh dear! What have I gotten myself into?" she cried as the door slammed behind her.

"This ain't no hotel deluxe—that's for sure," said Pedro the Chihuahua.

"Where ya been all my life, Honey?" asked the bulldog.

"Look at the collar—those gems ain't fakes. This dame's got dough," said Boris, the scrawny wolfhound.

"What'd you do? Give the maid fleas?" sneered the others.

"Oh come now fellas, leave the girl alone. Can't you see that the kid's got class?" said a floozy-looking female. "My name's Peg," she said to Lady. "What's yours?"

Lady introduced herself. "This Peg may not be a blushing violet," she thought, "but she certainly is kind."

"Don't worry, honey!" said Peg, winking. "Take it from someone who knows! A girl with your style won't stay here long."

Peg knew what she was talking about. Within a half hour, Lady was fetched by one of the guards and escorted home.

"So long, Duchess!" cried the dogs. "Don't forget us. Prison chains or house chains. They're all the same. Down with all chains!"

And speaking of chains, that's exactly what was waiting for Lady when she returned home. Aunt Sarah attached her to a doghouse by a short chain. She could barely move.

Jock and Trusty came to visit her. They felt sorry for the poor little dog. Lady was so ashamed she could barely speak.

Lady was sitting in the doghouse when she heard a familiar voice.

"Hi there Sweetie! What's new?"

It was Tramp, acting as if nothing had happened.

Forgetting that she was chained, Lady rushed out of her house and nearly choked herself. "Ah! So now you come!" she shrieked. "Have you no shame? How dare you come here after all that you've done! Look at me! This is all your fault!" The fur rose on Lady's back.

"But Sweetie..." Tramp began.

"And don't you call me Sweetie!" She snarled.

"But... but... let me explain," stammered Tramp.

"There's nothing to explain. Go away! I don't ever want to see you again!" Lady turned her back on him.

"What's eating her?" wondered Tramp as he slouched away with his tail between his legs. "She thinks I'm a good-for-nothing bum. How can I show her that I'm not such a bad guy? Now she'll never believe that I love her."

That night, as Lady lay crying in the doghouse, a big hairy rat was nearby, watching. He'd been waiting for her to go to sleep. He was thinking of the soft little baby upstairs. He couldn't wait to sink his teeth into the young flesh.

But Lady was too upset to sleep. She was feeling sad and lonely. She wished that Jim Dear and Darling would come back.

The rat couldn't wait any longer. He decided to take his chances!

Sniff! Sniff! "I can smell that baby from here," thought the rat. Climbing up a tree, he jumped onto the roof. He was slipping through the window when Lady saw him.

"Woof! Woof!" she barked, running out of her house. She'd forgotten about the chain and almost strangled herself.

Tramp, who'd been sulking nearby, came running.
"A rat!" cried Lady. "A big rat just went into the baby's
room!"

"Don't worry, Sweetie! I'll get him for you!" shouted
Tramp as he climbed into the house through a
downstairs window.

Aunt Sarah was woken by Lady's barking. "What's
that little pest up to now? If she keeps barking she's
going to wake the baby!" Aunt Sarah was furious. "I'll
teach her to wake everyone!"

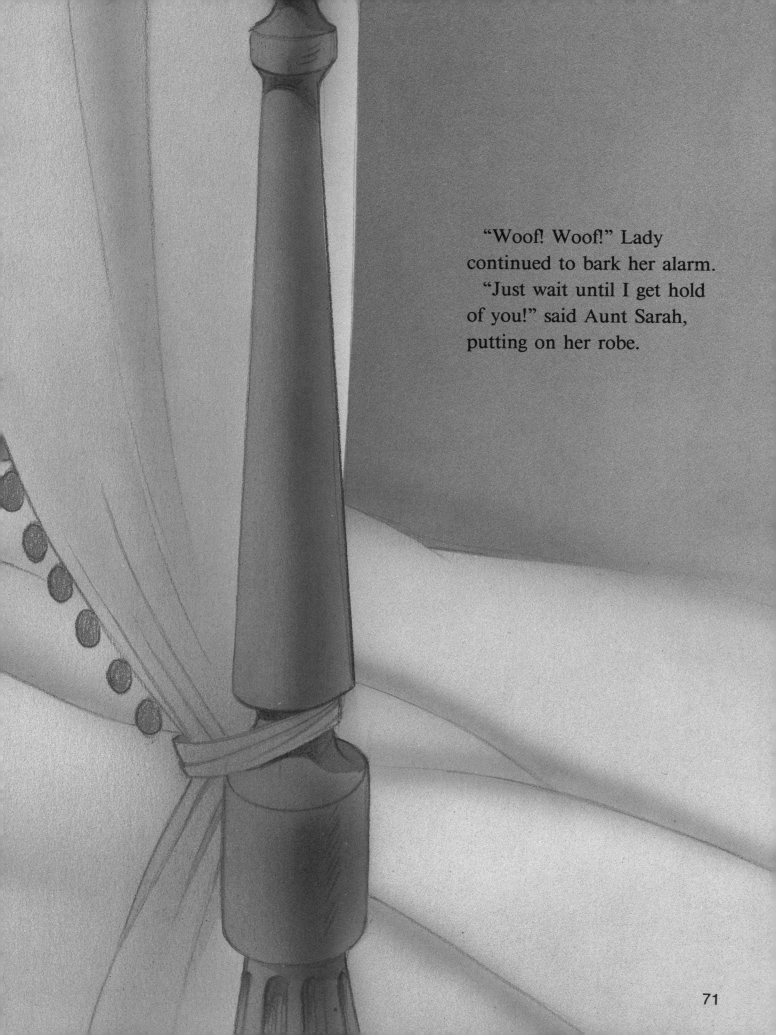

"Woof! Woof!" Lady
continued to bark her alarm.
"Just wait until I get hold
of you!" said Aunt Sarah,
putting on her robe.

Tramp finally reached the baby's room, and not a
minute too soon! The rat had climbed up above the
baby's crib and was ready to attack.

"GROWWL!" Tramp bared his teeth and jumped at
the rat. Startled, the rat lost its balance and fell to the
floor. Tramp jumped on it and the two began to fight!

Fur flew and teeth flashed
as the two rolled around the
floor. But the rat was no
match for the angry Tramp.
    Meanwhile Lady had
broken her chain and came
bounding into the room. She
saw the rat's body—it was
dead.

Lady looked at Tramp who was licking his wounds.
He was a bit scratched, but that was all.
The noise had wakened the baby who began to cry.
"WAAHH! WAAHHH!" The baby screamed at the top
of its lungs.

Lady was just about to thank Tramp when in stormed
Aunt Sarah. She was purple with rage and was carrying
a broom! She didn't see the dead rat. She had eyes only
for the two dogs.

"Out of here, you two! Down in the cellar! It's the dog
pound for you and this time forever!"

A swish of the broom and the two unlucky dogs found themselves pushed downstairs. The cellar door opened and they were thrust into the dark!

Suddenly, Lady heard familiar voices above. "It's Jim Dear and Darling! They've come home!" she told Tramp.

Within a few minutes the cellar door opened. "Lady! Here, Lady! Come on, girl!" called Jim Dear. Lady told Tramp to stay put and ran up the stairs into her master's arms. At the same time, two men from the dog pound crept down the stairs and grabbed Tramp. He was rushed into a waiting van.

Trusty and Jock saw him being driven away. "We must help the old fellow out," said Jock. "He may not be a gentleman, but he's a good dog!"

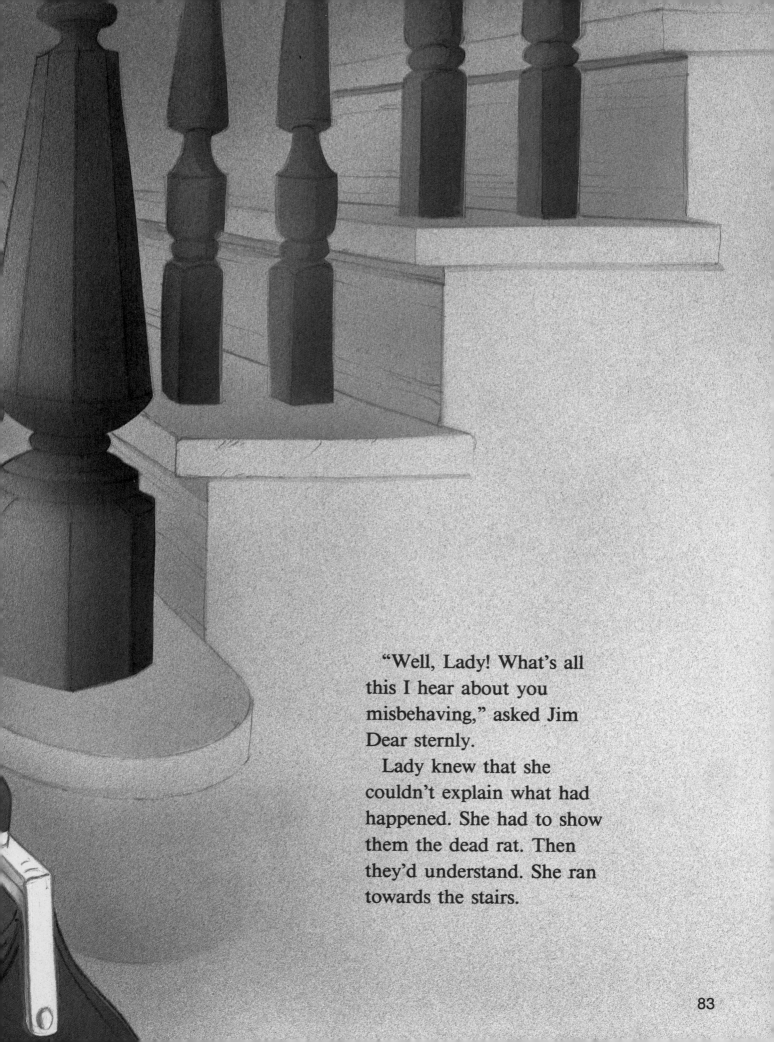

"Well, Lady! What's all this I hear about you misbehaving," asked Jim Dear sternly.

Lady knew that she couldn't explain what had happened. She had to show them the dead rat. Then they'd understand. She ran towards the stairs.

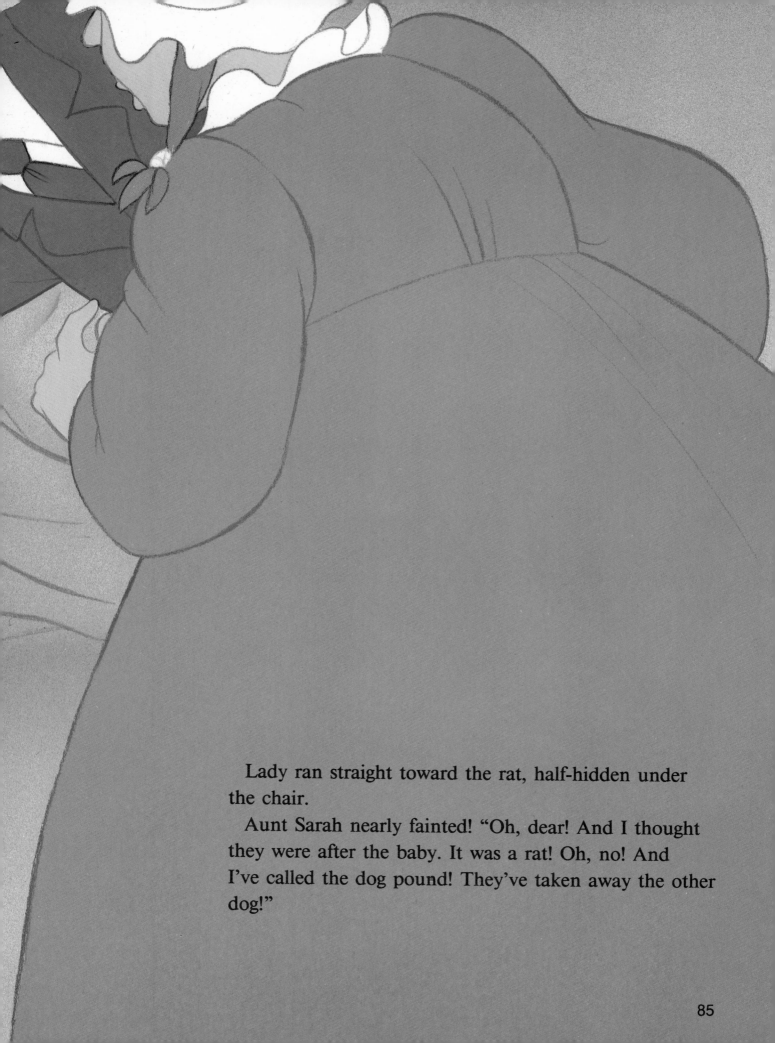

Lady ran straight toward the rat, half-hidden under the chair.

Aunt Sarah nearly fainted! "Oh, dear! And I thought they were after the baby. It was a rat! Oh, no! And I've called the dog pound! They've taken away the other dog!"

"Come with me, Lady!" shouted Jim Dear. "We'll find your friend. He saved my baby's life! It's the least we can do," He rushed down to find a cab.

But Lady was afraid that they'd be too late.

"Faster! Please hurry!" she cried as they sped toward the pound.

"He's no saint... he's not really handsome... he's even got fleas... but I love him all the same."

In the meantime, Trusty and Jock tracked down the
dog-pound carriage. Trusty wasn't so old after all! He
still knew a thing or two about detecting.

"I'll head him off," cried Trusty, running in front of
the horse. The frightened horse reared up and knocked
over the carriage.

Lady and Jim Dear had finally caught up with the
carriage. While Jim Dear talked to the driver, Lady ran
around to the back.

"Oh Tramp! Are you hurt?" asked Lady.

"Hi there, Sweetie! I'm just fine!" replied Tramp.
Nothing could harm that old scoundrel.

"Tell me something, Tramp," said Lady several weeks later. "What does a *bella fidanzata* mean?"

Tramp looked at Lady and grinned. "You've got a good memory, Sweetie! It means... um... a beautiful fiancée! And, that's what you are! Aren't you...?"

And so Lady and the Tramp became engaged and were soon married. Trusty, his leg in a bandage, but otherwise fine, and Jock, wearing his new plaid jacket, congratulated the happy couple.

"If it hadn't been for you, Trusty, I'd be dead. Thanks!" said Tramp.

"It was nothing, old man. All in a day's work," replied the proud Trusty.

Christmas Eve came again. But this time there were one... two... three... four puppies under the tree!

Produced by Twin Books
15 Sherwood Place
Greenwich, CT 06830
U.S.A.

This edition published in the USA for
K Mart Corporation
Troy, Michigan 48084

ISBN 0 86124 316 1

Printed in Hong Kong

Reprinted 1987